A

Animals

B

Baobab

c

Chobe

D

Delta

E

Elephants

F

Francistown

G

Gaborone

H

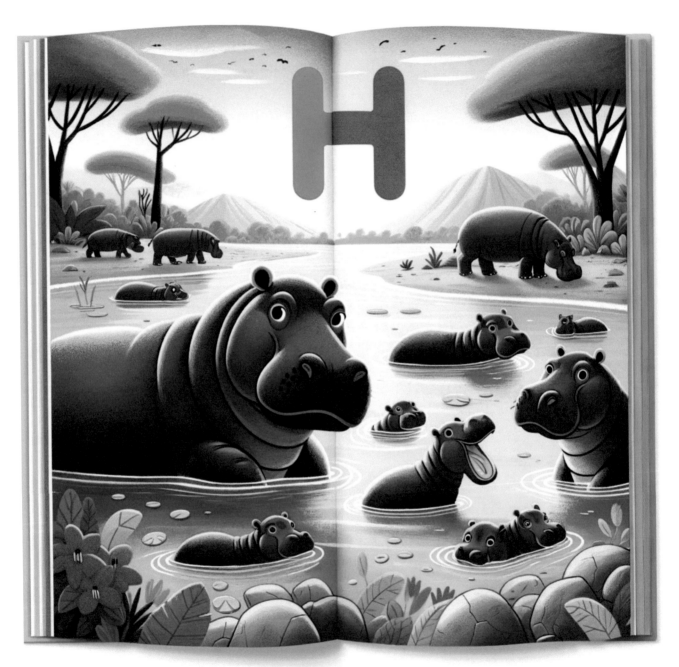

Hippo

I

Impala

J

Jewelry

K

Kalahari Desert

L

Leopard

M

Meerkat

N

Nata

O

Oryx.

P

Pula

Q

Quiver Tree

R

Rhino

S

Safari

T

Tsodilo

U

Umbrella Thorn

V

Vulture

W

Waterlily

X

Xigera

Y

Yellow Mongoose

z

Z

Zebra

Now It's Your Turn!

Can you spot the zebra's stripes? What colors do you see?

What animals are hiding near the waterlily pond?

Can you find the yellow mongoose? What is it doing in the savannah?

Made in United States
Troutdale, OR
10/01/2024

23302624R00017